Contents

Disney

ANNUAL 2006

Pedigree®

Published by Pedigree Books Limited
Beech Hill House, Walnut Gardens, Exeter, Devon, EX4 4DH
Email: books@pedigreegroup.co.uk
Under licence from Disney   © Disney 2005

£7.99

HE'S INCREDIBLY INTELLIGENT AND NEARLY *INDESTRUCTIBLE*...

...BUT THERE *MUST* BE A WAY TO STOP HIM!

MAYBE I SHOULD MAKE *SANDWICHES*.

HE *LOVES* MY SANDWICHES!

IF THE *GALACTIC FEDERATION* FINDS OUT *I* CREATED THAT LITTLE BLUE MENACE, I'LL BE *RUINED!*

UNAWARE THAT HIS CREATOR IS CLOSING IN ON HIM, STITCH CONTINUES TO *MISBEHAVE*

SKRUNCH

STITCH HAS BROKEN INTO THE PET STORE AND LET ALL THE ANIMALS LOOSE!

626 HAS BROKEN STRAIGHT THROUGH TO THE *MUSEUM OF GALACTIC SCIENCE!*

HEY, NOT *ME!*

TELL HIM I'M NOT A *SPACE PET,* DOC!

YOU *WILL* END UP AS SOMEBODY'S SPACE PET IF YOU DON'T START *HELPING!*

SPACE PETS

CAT ON MY HEAD!

SPACE CAT ON MY HEAD!

YOU HAVE TO HAND IT TO 626...

...AS A *TROUBLEMAKER* HE'S GOT STYLE *AND* IMAGINATION.

7

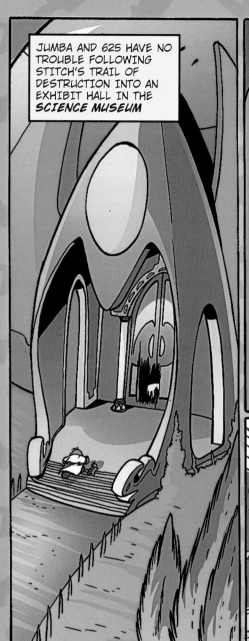

JUMBA AND 625 HAVE NO TROUBLE FOLLOWING STITCH'S TRAIL OF DESTRUCTION INTO AN EXHIBIT HALL IN THE **SCIENCE MUSEUM**

HE'S **ACTIVATED** THE ORBITING **MODEL GALAXY!**

HELP ME FIND THE **CONTROLS!**

DO WE **HAVE** TO STOP IT?

THAT THING IS **COOL!**

THE MISCHIEVOUS STITCH SWINGS ONE OF THE PLANETS OUT OF ITS **ORBIT** — WITH SPECTACULAR RESULTS!

UH, YOU **SURE** YOU KNOW WHAT YOU'RE DOING, DOC?

BAH! OF COURSE I DO.

WHY, THIS CONTROL PANEL IS **SO** SIMPLE, A **BABY** COULD FIGURE IT OUT!

EEEP!

DANGER MODEL SPEED CRITICAL!!

MAYBE I SHOULD GO FIND A BABY, HUH?

THE ROTATION IS OUT OF CONTROL!

LET'S GET OUT OF HERE, 625!

IN SECONDS, THE PLANET'S SPEED REACHES *BREAKING POINT* — GIVING STITCH THE RIDE OF HIS LIFE!

KER-RRRRASH!

WELL, THAT WENT BETTER THAN I EXPECTED.

QUICK — WE MUST LEAVE BEFORE WE'RE *CAUGHT!*

WHAT ABOUT *626?*

WE'LL CATCH UP WITH HIM LATER!

BY MY CALCULATIONS, HE SHOULD HAVE BEEN FLUNG *VERY* FAR FROM HERE!

'VERY FAR'? ARE YOU *SURE* YOU'RE A SCIENTIST?

YOU ARE A *MISERABLE* EXCUSE FOR AN EXPERIMENT, 625.

THE END

DISNEY'S **KIM POSSIBLE** — *Moon Shot*

BREAKFAST AT THE KIM POSSIBLE HOUSE IS INTERRUPTED BY...

HI, WADE, WHAT'S THE SITCH?

BAD NEWS, KIM...

...MY COMPUTER'S JUST FLAGGED AN UNUSUAL ORDER FOR ASTROTURF! BY MY CALCULATIONS IT'S ENOUGH TO COVER A SPHERICAL OBJECT 2,160 MILES IN DIAMETER!

NO IDEA WHAT IT MEANS BUT I FIGURE IT'S JUST ODD ENOUGH TO SMELL LIKE A RAT!

THANKS, WADE.

HMM, WONDER WHO'D ORDER THAT MUCH ARTIFICIAL GRASS...

ENOUGH TO COVER THE MOON!

EXACTLY!

YES, *EXACTLY*!

2,160 MILES IS THE PRECISE DIAMETER OF THE MOON, KIMMY. SOUNDS TO ME LIKE SOMEONE'S PLANNING...

YOU MEAN, *ACTUALLY* EXACTLY? WHOA!

"...TO ASTROTURF THE MOON!"

THANKS FOR THE LIFT, GUYS.

AFTER YOU SAVED OUR SPACE STATION FROM MELTDOWN LAST MONTH, IT'S THE LEAST WE COULD DO.

HEY, NO BIGGY!

WOW! HAVING A ROCKET-SCIENTIST DAD REALLY PAYS OFF SOMETIMES. HEY, THERE'S THE ARTIFICIAL GRASS WADE TOLD ME ABOUT...

... IF YOU CAN MAKE A BETTER SHOT THAN ME, I'LL GIVE UP MY PLAN AND COME QUIETLY. DEAL?

WHATEVER!

GOOD! BECAUSE I NEVER LOSE!

HOLE IN ONE! OH NO!

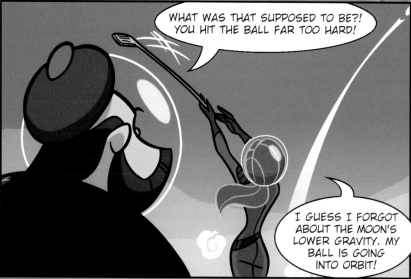

WHAT WAS THAT SUPPOSED TO BE?! YOU HIT THE BALL FAR TOO HARD!

I GUESS I FORGOT ABOUT THE MOON'S LOWER GRAVITY. MY BALL IS GOING INTO ORBIT!

WITH THE MOON'S LIGHTER GRAVITY, THE BALL CONTINUES TO TRAVEL ALL THE WAY AROUND THE MOON...

...UNTIL IT CATCHES UP WITH DUFF KILLAGAN...

YOWCH!

THAT *PUTT* DUFF IN HIS PLACE!

THE END

Disney
Mickey's Christmas Carol

Good day to you all! I'm Bob Cratchit, from a company called Scrooge and Cratchit.
Mr. Scrooge and I have been in business together for some time now, but it wasn't always
that way. In fact, Ebenezer Scrooge used to be the greediest miser in the land and I was
nothing more than his underpaid, overworked clerk. It all changed one Christmas...

It was Christmas Eve. Ebenezer Scrooge trudged through the snow to his counting house, scowling at the seasonal jollity around him.

"Merry Christmas to one and all!" a carol singer cheerfully called out to him. Scrooge ignored him and marched on past a group of beggars huddled round a small fire.

"Will you give a penny for the poor, gov'nor?" one of them asked hopefully, holding out a grubby hand.

"Bah!" Scrooge replied, waving him away. Reaching his office, he banged the snow off the sign with his stick. The company used to be known as Scrooge and Marley, but Marley's name was now crossed out.

"Dead seven years now," Scrooge said to himself, remembering his old business partner. "But he was a goodun – he robbed from the widows and swindled the poor!" Chuckling to himself, he pushed the door open and went inside.

"G-g-good morning, Mr. Scrooge," stuttered his clerk, Bob Cratchit, standing by the stove and hiding something behind his back. There was no fooling his boss, though. "What are you doing with that piece of coal, Cratchit?" he snapped.

"I just wanted to thaw the ink," sighed Bob. Scrooge was so mean that sometimes the room was cold enough to freeze the ink solid. He reminded Bob that he had used a piece of coal the previous week and ordered him to get on with his work.

"I was wondering," Bob said brightly, "since tomorrow is Christmas, might I have a half day off?"

"I suppose so," grumbled Scrooge, "but I'll have to dock your pay!" Before Bob could reply, the door swung open and Fred, Scrooge's nephew, strode in and wished them both a merry Christmas.

"What's so merry about it?" his uncle snapped. "It's just another working day!"

Fred had come to invite his uncle to Christmas lunch, but Scrooge refused, chasing him away.

"Bah, humbug!" he muttered, turning to count his money. At the sound of the door opening, he turned back and made an effort to look welcoming.

"Ah, customers!" he smiled. But the visitors were not customers; they were charity collectors asking for money to help the poor.

"But if you give money to the poor, they won't be poor anymore," Scrooge told them, "and if they're not poor anymore, you won't need to collect for them. If you can't collect for them, you won't have a job!"

Scrooge ushered his visitors out, saying he would hate to put them out of a job at Christmas time. In fact, he could have spared a penny or two, but he did not see why he should work all his life for money, only to give it away.

Bob tried to explain that Christmas was a time for giving, but Scrooge was having none of it. Even Christmas cheer could not thaw the old miser's icy heart. He sat counting and calculating for the rest of the day with no more mention of the festive season.

Blowing on his cold, numb hands that evening, Bob glanced at the clock: it was exactly seven o'clock. As he got up to go, Scrooge stopped him.

"That's two minutes fast," he said, checking the time on his pocket watch. Bob wearily sat down again. "But never mind the two minutes," added Scrooge. "You may go."

"Oh, thank you, sir!" exclaimed Bob, jumping out of his seat. "You're so kind!"

"Never mind the mushy stuff," grumbled Scrooge. "Just go home."

Bob went, but could not help wishing Scrooge a merry Christmas before he left.

"Bah, humbug!" came the usual reply.

Scrooge worked for a further two hours before locking up his counting house to go home. He plodded through the snow, hunched against the cold and ignoring the sounds of celebration that drifted from the houses he passed. As he reached his own front door and turned the key, the doorknocker seemed to look like his old partner and he even thought he heard his voice.

"Marley?" he whispered, blinking in disbelief. "It can't be," he added, shaking his head and going inside. Slamming the door behind him, Scrooge stood in the hallway, afraid to go up the stairs. He crept up the first few and was sure he heard the sound of chains clinking. Stopping to listen more carefully, he felt as if his hat were being lifted from his head, but still told himself he was imagining things. He hurried to his bedroom and locked the door.

A locked door, of course, is no obstacle for a ghost. Even so, the ghost knocked before appearing through it and calling Scrooge's name. Terrified, Scrooge hid his head under a cushion and trembled with fear.

"Don't you recognise me, Scrooge?" the ghost asked, kindly. "It's me, Jacob Marley. I was your partner, remember?"

Scrooge sat up and looked in amazement.

"Jacob? It's really you!" he exclaimed.

"I'm here to give you a warning," said Marley. "I was wrong to rob from widows and swindle the poor when I was alive. As punishment, I must carry these heavy chains for eternity...or maybe even longer! The same will happen to you."

"It can't, it mustn't!" said Scrooge, panic-stricken. Marley told him that he should listen to the three spirits who would visit him that night if he wanted to escape the same fate.

Once the ghost had gone, dragging his chains behind him, Scrooge fell exhausted into bed and went straight to sleep. It was not long before he was awoken by the sound of a bell. He peeped through the curtains of his bed to see a tiny spirit, no more than a few inches high.

"Who are you?" Scrooge asked.

"I'm the Ghost of Christmas Past," came the reply. "Your past."

The spirit opened the window, letting in a blast of icy air. Putting up his little umbrella, he told Scrooge to come with him: they were going to visit the past. Scrooge held on and they flew out of the window through the snow, over the rooftops and past clouds of chimney smoke. Eventually they came down outside a building that Scrooge recognised as his first workplace.

"It's Fezziwig's!" he exclaimed. "I couldn't have worked for a kinder man."

Scrooge gazed through the window at the lively Christmas party inside and saw himself there as a happy young man.

"That's me!" he gasped. "They were my dearest friends."

"That was before you became a miser, consumed with greed," the spirit said, sternly.

Scrooge looked back and smiled as he saw the person he had loved more than anyone: Isabel. They were dancing happily together, but then the picture changed. Suddenly, he was in his counting house, telling Isabel that she owed him money on a cottage that he would have to take from her. Isabel was sobbing: with that cruel act, he had broken her heart.

"You loved your gold more than Isabel," sighed the spirit, "and you lost her forever."

Scrooge could not bear to see any more of these painful memories and begged the spirit to take him back home.

In his bed Scrooge was wondering how he could have been so foolish, when he was startled by a booming voice that called: "Fee fi fo fum, I smell a stingy Englishman!" Scrooge was astonished to see the spirit of a giant in his room, surrounded by mounds of delicious Christmas food. Spotting Scrooge, the giant picked him up and peered at him.

"I am the Ghost of Christmas Present," he said, "and this is the food of generosity that you have long denied your fellow men."

The giant carried Scrooge to the Cratchits' house to see the meagre Christmas meal that the family would have that day. Scrooge was saddened to see that the youngest son, Tiny Tim, was crippled and walked with a crutch. The youngster seemed delighted at the miniature portion of food put before him and Scrooge noticed that Bob's plate held even less.

The Ghost of Christmas Present told Scrooge that Tiny Tim was very ill and that if things did not change soon, his chair would be empty at the next Christmas meal. "W-what do you mean by that?" asked Scrooge, as the scene disappeared before him, but the spirit had gone. An icy mist swirled around him and he realised that he was in a graveyard. A shadowy figure loomed over him and he shrank away from it, knowing that it must be the third spirit.

"Are you the Ghost of Christmas Future?" he whispered. "Please...tell me what becomes of Tiny Tim."

The spirit pointed silently to a grave in the distance: beside it stood the Cratchits. Bob tearfully put the little crutch against Tiny Tim's headstone while his grief-stricken wife comforted their sobbing children.

"No!" cried Scrooge. "Please, spirit. Tell me that these events can yet be changed!"

Scrooge was distracted by the sound of chuckling nearby. It was gravediggers,

taking a break from shovelling earth on to a coffin in the ground. He heard them say

that not one person had come to the funeral earlier. Curious, Scrooge crept towards

the hole.

"Whose lonely grave is this?" he asked the spirit, peering into it.

"Yours!" cackled the Ghost of Christmas Future, pushing him over the edge.

"Ebenezer Scrooge, the richest man in the cemetery!"

As Scrooge fell towards the coffin, it seemed to burst into flames.

"No!" he cried, struggling to clamber out of the grave. "I'll change! I'll change…"

He called out over and over again until he realised he was back in his bedroom,

entangled in his bedcovers. Hurrying over to the window, he flung it open to see that

it was a crisp, sunny Christmas morning: the spirits had given him another chance.

Scrooge was so relieved to find things back to normal that he pulled on his coat and rushed outside, still in his nightgown and slippers. Cackling to himself, he slid down the snowy handrail and ran into the two collectors for the poor. He opened his coat to reveal pockets full of bulging moneybags and handed over two of them.

"Here," he smiled. "A hundred gold pieces. Merry Christmas to one and all!"

"One hundred gold pieces?" the pair echoed in disbelief. Was this really the same Scrooge who had sent them away empty-handed only a day ago? They watched in amazement as he skipped off down the street, wishing passers-by a merry Christmas.

"Ah, nephew!" he called out to Fred, who was passing in his horse-drawn cart. "I'm looking forward to that wonderful meal later!"

Fred waved back in reply, puzzled but delighted by his uncle's change of heart.

Scrooge bounded down the high street and called into the butcher's shop, announcing that he would have the biggest turkey they had left. His next visit was to the toyshop, where he bought enough toys to fill a large sack. He hurried to the Cratchits' house with it thrown over his shoulder and knocked on the door.

"Mr. Scrooge!" exclaimed Bob, surprised to see him. "Please, come in."

Scrooge pretended to be his old grumpy self to begin with and Bob thought the sack would be full of the laundry that he sometimes had to do as part of his job. The whole family gasped when Scrooge opened it, revealing the turkey and gifts that were inside. He smiled as the children scrabbled excitedly to open the presents.

"What's more," he added, "I've decided to give you a raise and make you my partner in the business! Merry Christmas, Bob!"

So it came to be that Ebenezer Scrooge, the meanest of misers, spent Christmas
morning playing with the Cratchit children instead of grumbling alone in his gloomy
house. Bob and his wife looked fondly upon the scene, knowing that from that day on,
their life would no longer be one of poverty and hardship. Scrooge went on to join his
nephew and other family members for his first Christmas dinner in years. They
welcomed him so warmly that he wondered why he had so often wanted to miss it.

Scrooge's newfound kindness continued for the rest of his days. He saw to it that
the Cratchits, especially Tiny Tim, never wanted for anything and he became friends
with all who lived in the town. Every Christmas, he was generous with his hospitality
and his gifts to the poor. Needless to say, he never saw the three spirits again...

Disney's Treasure Planet

"The Trouble With Pirates!"

PIRATES!

DON'T LET HIM GET **AWAY**, YOU SWABS! THAT BOY IS ONTO OUR **PLANS**!

I'VE SPENT ALL THESE YEARS LIVING ON THE MOST **BORING** PLANET IN THE GALAXY, HOPING SOMETHING-- **ANYTHING**--INTERESTING WOULD HAPPEN.

BUT BEING CHASED BY BLOODTHIRSTY PIRATES WASN'T EXACTLY WHAT I HAD IN MIND!

HOW DID I **EVER** GET MYSELF INTO THIS **MESS**?

DON'T WORRY, CAP'N--HE WON'T TELL A **LIVING** SOUL!

THE PLANET MONTRESSOR-- THE DULL ROUTINE OF **JIM HAWKINS'** LIFE ON THIS REMOTE MINING PLANET HAS JUST BEEN SHATTERED! THANKS TO HIS RESTLESS CURIOSITY, JIM FINDS HIMSELF ON THE RUN FROM RUTHLESS PIRATES ABOARD HIS SOARING **SOLAR SURFER**!

FLASHBACK!

TO DISCOVER JUST HOW JIM DID END UP IN SUCH A DANGEROUS FIX, WE MUST LOOK BACK TO EVENTS WHICH OCCURRED EARLIER THAT DAY AT THE **BENBOW INN**...

I JUST DON'T KNOW WHAT TO DO ABOUT JIM, **DR. DOPPLER.**

EVER SINCE HIS FATHER LEFT US HE'S BEEN SO... **MOODY.**

AND LATELY HE'S BEEN GETTING INTO... TROUBLE.

TRY TO BE PATIENT WITH HIM, **SARAH.**

IT ISN'T EASY FOR A BOY TO GROW UP WITHOUT A FATHER.

BOP-DA-DIDDLY-BOP-YEEH!

OH, BROTHER! HAVE YOU GONE COMPLETELY NUTS, TIMON?

SCAT-DOO-BOOP-BEEEE-BAAAAHH!

WHAT *ARE* YOU DOING? APART FROM LOOKING *DUMB*?

DUMB? I'M LOOKING COOL! AND THIS IS WHAT'LL FEED US FROM NOW ON!

WE'LL SING FOR OUR SUPPER! AND AS OUR REPUTATION SPREADS, JUNGLE FOLK EVERYWHERE'LL COLLECT FOOD FOR US!

YEAH? AND *WHY* WOULD THEY DO THAT?

ISN'T IT OBVIOUS, KNUCKLE-HEAD? WE'LL SING AND SANCE, FOLK'LL LOVE IT AND THEY'LL FEED US! NOW LET'S GET REHEARSING!

ME?! *SING?!* IF THEY HEAR MY HORRIBLE VOICE, THEY'LL ALL LEAVE!

AND PUMBAA'S NOT KIDDING

WAILLLLLL-SNORRRRT-YERRRRRKKK-WHOOOOO!

MMM! NEEDS SOME WORK! BUT WE'LL GET THERE IN THE END!

OWUUUUULL-EEEEEEEKKK-BURRRRPP!

PERSIST, KIDDO! ONE DAY THIS IDEA WILL SWEEP THE WORLD!

AFTER MANY HOURS OF PRACTICE

SHUCKS. TIMON! CAN'T WE JUST STICK TO REGULAR GRUB-GRABBING?

LET'S GO! FAME, FORTUNE AND LOTS OF GRUBS AWAIT US!

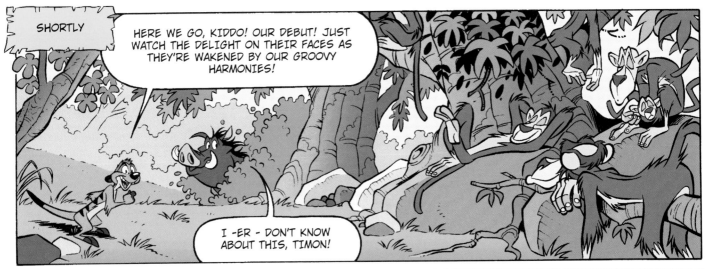

SHORTLY

HERE WE GO, KIDDO! OUR DEBUT! JUST WATCH THE DELIGHT ON THEIR FACES AS THEY'RE WAKENED BY OUR GROOVY HARMONIES!

I -ER - DON'T KNOW ABOUT THIS, TIMON!

WAAAAAHHHHHHH!

OOMMPPPHH! HONNNKK!! HONNKK!

SCAT-OOBLY-DOOO! DEE-DAH!

HUH?!

EH?!

AFTER 'EM! GIVE 'EM A WHACKING!

SEE? WHAT DID I TELL YOU?

WAKE OUR BABIES WITH YOUR RACKET, WOULD YOU

SHUT UP, PUMBBA, AND GET IN HERE QUICK!

RIGHT BEHIND YOU!

WE DON'T WANT THEM TO FIND US, SO JUST KEEP QUIET WILL YOU, PUMBAA!

THAT'S WHAT I'VE BEEN TELLING YOU ALL ALONG! I SHOULD BE QUIET, AND NOT *SINGING*!

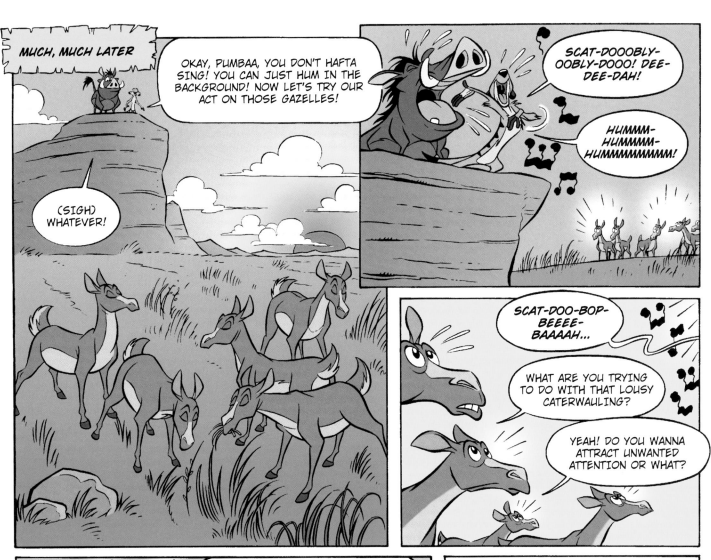

OKAY, PUMBAA, YOU DON'T HAFTA SING! YOU CAN JUST HUM IN THE BACKGROUND! NOW LET'S TRY OUR ACT ON THOSE GAZELLES!

(SIGH) WHATEVER!

SCAT-DOOOBLY-OOBLY-DOOO! DEE-DEE-DAH!

HUMMM-HUMMMM-HUMMMMMMMM!

SCAT-DOO-BOP-BEEEE-BAAAAH...

WHAT ARE YOU TRYING TO DO WITH THAT LOUSY CATERWAULING?

YEAH! DO YOU WANNA ATTRACT UNWANTED ATTENTION OR WHAT?

YIKES! YOUR RIGHT! RUN FOR IT, FELLAS, A COUPLE OF LEOPARDS ARE CREEPING UP ON YOU!

GOTCHA! WE'RE OUTTA HERE!

AT LEAST WE'RE SAFE FOR THE MEANTIME, PUMBAA! BUT I GUESS WE SHOULD TRY TO FIND REFUGE SOMEWHERE!

(SIGH) YEAH!

I'M STARVING! SO FROM KNOW ON I'M GONNA HUNT MY OWN FOOD!

BUT I STILL THINK IT'S A GOOD IDEA! ONE DAY FOLKS'LL SING AN' DANCE, AND OTHERS'LL PAY LOTSA GRUBS TO SEE 'EM DO IT! MAKE MY WORDS!

chicken little

This was the proudest moment of Chicken Little's life: he and his dad were settling down at the cinema to watch a very special film. It was special because the hero was Chicken Little himself! The film told the story of how this brave little chicken saved his home town of Oakey Oaks...

It was a normal, sunny day in the little town of Oakey Oaks. Chicken Little was sitting happily under a tree when BONK! Something fell on his head!

"The sky is falling!" he gasped. He raced up to the school bell tower and frantically swung from the bell's rope.

"Run for your lives!" the tiny chicken shrieked down to the townspeople. "You're all in danger! The sky is falling!"

Everyone ran...into phone poles, into trees and into each other. Chicken Little led a panic-stricken crowd to the tree, but there was nothing there. He pointed to a stop sign and told everyone that the piece of sky had been the same shape.

"There's been a mistake," interrupted Buck Cluck. "It was just an acorn that hit him. Sorry, folks." Chicken Little was very upset. Even his dad didn't believe him!

A year later, as Buck drove Chicken Little to the school bus stop, they saw a poster for 'Crazy Little Chicken: The Movie'. Buck groaned. His son had made one mistake and everyone was still talking about it.

"Remember how I told you it would be better for you to lie low?" he asked his son gently. "Don't draw attention to yourself, right?"

Chicken Little had other ideas, but his dad wouldn't listen to him. After being dropped off, Chicken Little went to the bus stop. In the rush for the school bus, he was trampled by his classmates and missed it. As he struggled to get up, the school bully, Foxy Loxy, leaned out of the bus window and tossed some acorns in front of him. He skidded on them and tumbled to the ground.

Chicken Little raced towards school, still determined to get there on time.

As he was crossing the road, Chicken Little fell on a piece of bubble gum and, being so tiny, was stuck fast. The smart chicken pulled out a lollipop, licked it, and stuck it to the bumper of a passing car, hitching a ride. Unfortunately, his shorts were still stuck to the gum! Now there was another challenge: how to get into class without being seen in his underpants.

After hiding behind bushes on his way to school, Chicken Little had another idea. He shook up a bottle of fizzy pop and attached it to his back, using it as a rocket to launch himself into the window of his school. He raced to his locker and jumped inside, where he made himself a pair of shorts from a piece of paper. He hurried to his gym class to join his friends Fish, Abby and Runt for a game of dodgeball.

During the game, Foxy Loxy threw the ball in Abby's face.

"That does it!" Chicken Little bravely marched up to the bully. "Prepare to hurt!"

Foxy snapped her fingers. Goosey Loosey instantly appeared and slung the chicken up against the window. After a moment, he slowly slid down the glass and grabbed on to the first thing he could to stop his fall. It was the fire alarm.

BRRRRRING! The alarm and the sprinklers went off. Everyone got soaked and Chicken Little's paper shorts fell apart. For the second time that day, he was in his underpants. Buck Cluck was called. He brought Chicken Little a new pair of shorts and went to talk to the principal while his son waited by the door.

"Ever since that sky-falling incident, he's been nothing but trouble!" the principal exclaimed. With a sigh, Chicken Little looked at the trophy case on the wall. Some of the awards were his father's.

Buck Cluck had been the town's baseball champion in his day. Looking at his trophies gave Chicken Little an idea: he could make himself into a baseball hero! That would make up for his mistake and his dad would be proud of him at last.

"Um, hey, Dad? I was thinking," he began in the car on the way home, "what if I joined the baseball team?"

Buck Cluck swerved the car in surprise.

"Son, I'm just wondering...maybe baseball isn't exactly your thing, you know?" he reasoned. "Have you considered the chess team?"

Chicken Little had made up his mind. He was determined to put things right and so he joined The Acorns baseball team. Game after game, he waited to play, but always ended up on the bench. It seemed as if he would never get a chance to change his life...until The Acorns made it to the big game.

"Yes, it's been two decades since The Acorns have beaten rivals The Spud Valley Taters," shouted the announcer. "Hopefully, there's enough muscle on the bench to pull out a win. Up next, Chicken Little." The Oakey Oaks crowd stopped in mid-cheer. Chicken Little?!

"He's gonna lose the game for us!" gasped one fan. Chicken Little went to bat. He was determined to make his dad proud.

"Today is a new day," he whispered to himself. Summoning all his strength, he swung the heavy bat – and hit the ball! For a moment he was too surprised to move, then he raced around the bases and slid into home...just as one of the Taters tagged him out.

"Wait!" shouted the umpire. He swept away the dust to find that Chicken Little's foot was touching home plate. "The runner is safe!"

Chicken Little had won the big game for The Acorns!

When they got home, Buck and Chicken Little replayed the game in his room. Chicken Little slid into their makeshift home plate while Buck pretended to catch the ball. "The mighty Acorns win!" Buck cheered. Then he flopped down on to his son's bed. "I guess that puts the whole 'sky is falling' incident behind us once and for all, kiddo!" "You bet, Dad!" agreed Chicken Little. He truly felt that this was a new start. After Buck said goodnight, Chicken Little gazed happily out at the stars. One of them seemed especially big and there was something strange about it. He took off his glasses, cleaned them, put them back on and looked again. It was getting bigger! BOOM! The star flew through the window and landed on Chicken Little. When he was finally able to stand up, all he could do was shout, "NOOOOOO!"

Buck raced upstairs and opened the door. Chicken Little managed to hide the piece of star just in time by throwing a blanket over it.

"Hey, what's wrong?" Buck asked. "I thought I heard you yell."

"I, uh, fell out of bed," Chicken Little replied. He couldn't bear to say that the sky had fallen on him again. When his dad had gone he moved the blanket, but the star panel had disappeared!

Chicken Little soon realised that the star panel hadn't really vanished: it had blended into the floor. Picking it up, he saw that the back was covered with lights and wires. The front took on the appearance of whatever it stood against. Chicken Little held it up to the window and it looked like...part of the sky.

"Oh, no!" he groaned. The sky really had fallen on him again!

Chicken Little called Abby, Runt and Fish and asked them to come to his house quickly. He showed them the strange object and told them how it had landed on him from nowhere. Fish began playing with it, while Abby said Chicken Little should talk to his dad. But the chicken simply couldn't.

"There is no way I'm bringing up any sky falling stuff with him again," he said firmly. Just then, Fish pressed a button on the panel and it began to float. He happily jumped on board and zoomed around the room on it. Abby, Runt and Chicken Little watched in disbelief as the panel flew out of the window with Fish delightedly waving to them with his light stick. As he flew up into the darkness, all his friends could see was the glow from his stick. They ran out of the room and downstairs: they had to save their friend!

Chicken Little, Abby and Runt raced after Fish, scrambling over fences and running across gardens with their eyes glued to the sky. At last, Fish's light stick came to a stop over the town's baseball field.

"Hold on, Fish!" shouted Runt. "We will save you!"

Suddenly, dust and leaves swirled around them and a bright circle lit up the night sky. It was a spaceship, coming down to land in the middle of the ball field! Chicken Little and his friends dashed to the dugout to hide. They watched as with a hiss, the door on the ship slid open and two giant, spider-like aliens floated out. Abby gasped and pointed towards the ship. From inside, Fish was waving to them. Chicken Little took a deep breath. There was only one way that they could save Fish now: they would have to board the spaceship.

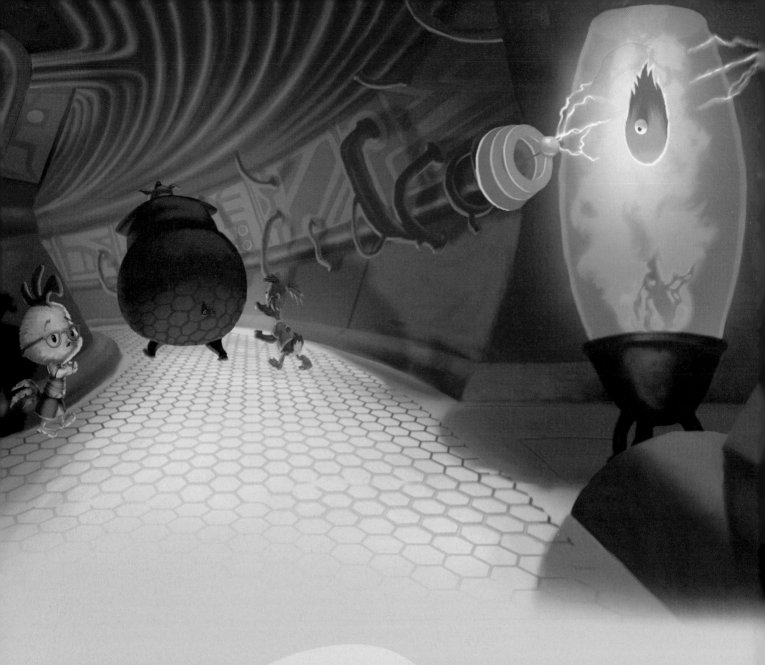

When the aliens were out of sight, Chicken Little, Abby and Runt slipped into the spaceship and tiptoed down a dim corridor. Chicken Little noticed a furry, orange creature inside a blue capsule. As he stared at it curiously, he saw its eye pop open. He winked...and it winked back! Frightened, Chicken Little turned away and caught up with his friends, not seeing that the thing had sprouted little legs, jumped down and followed him.

"Fish!" Abby cried out. "What have they done to you?" She had spotted Fish's skeleton at the end of the corridor and began to run towards him. Runt could hardly bear to look and had to breathe into paper bags to help his panic attack. Then, completely unharmed, Fish stepped out from behind an x-ray screen and waved cheerfully. He seemed as happy as ever, thrilled by his latest adventure!

Fish was fine...but Earth was not! In the next room, the four friends found a map with other planets crossed off and Earth circled.

"It looks like we're next," Chicken Little gulped. They all dashed towards the hatch to escape.

"We're running back to your house and you're going to tell your dad!" Abby told Chicken Little. This time, he agreed.

When the aliens saw that the fuzzy creature was missing from its capsule, they seemed alarmed. They began to chase after Chicken Little and his friends, who ran as fast as they could towards the exit. Runt needed some help from Abby to get through the hatch, while Chicken Little struggled to keep a door closed with the aliens on the other side. Soon all four friends were outside. They raced out of the baseball stadium and into the woods with the aliens following close behind.

At the edge of the woods, the group of friends tumbled down a hill and into a cornfield, where they scrambled to hide among the cornstalks. In all the commotion, neither the aliens nor Chicken Little and his friends noticed the little orange creature from the spaceship. He watched everything from afar, with his three eyes wide open. For a moment or two, as the friends huddled amongst the corn, it seemed as if they had escaped the aliens...until they heard a loud buzzing noise. They looked up and were horrified to see that the aliens had transformed their tentacles into huge, sharp blades that whirred as they sliced through the cornstalks in search of the group. Terrified, the friends raced towards their school. If they could just get to the bell and ring it, they could warn the people of Oakey Oaks that aliens were attacking!

The aliens were closing in on the friends and unfortunately the door to the school was locked. Thinking quickly, Chicken Little used his fizz-rocket know-how to blast himself up to the bell rope. Just as he caught it, he remembered ringing this same bell and shouting that the sky was falling...it had been his big mistake. Chicken Little froze. He couldn't ring the bell. Not again. Then Abby screamed: the aliens had caught up with them!

Chicken Little had to save his friends; he gave the bell a mighty tug and rang it again and again. Strangely enough, the aliens ran away. The sound seemed to hurt their ears! Meanwhile, everyone in Oakey Oaks rushed to the school to see what was going on. Chicken Little was afraid of what they would think if he told them the truth, so he yelled, "Just come to the ball field!"

Chicken Little led the worried townspeople to the baseball stadium.

"Hurry!" he shouted on the way. The spaceship was starting to take off, and no one was there to see it! By the time everyone arrived at the field, the spaceship had completely disappeared, blending into the night sky until it was completely hidden.

"There was a spaceship here!" Chicken Little told the crowd. "And now it's invisible – it's made of special stuff that blends into the sky!" Abby said she had seen it, too, but no one believed them.

"It's that acorn thing all over again," someone grumbled. Chicken Little turned to his father.

"Dad, I'm not making this up!" he said. "You have to believe me this time."

"No, son," sighed Buck Cluck. "I don't. I can't tell you how embarrassed I am, folks," he added, facing the crowd. Chicken Little was devastated.

Meanwhile, the furry creature from the spaceship crouched, hidden and alone, and watched his spaceship streak across the night sky. His parents had left without him! Looking around, he caught sight of Chicken Little. He decided to follow him because he recognised him from the spaceship – and because he didn't know where else to go.

The next day was not a happy one in the Cluck household. Buck frantically answered telephone calls as the whole town called to complain about his son. As he apologised over and over again, Chicken Little slunk outside and sat down glumly. He had lost all the glory of the baseball game and was once again the laughing-stock of Oakey Oaks, just as he had been for the past year. His friends came and tried to cheer him up. "If ever there was a time to talk to your dad," Abby said, "it's now."

Chicken Little wanted to be alone so he could think about what to do next. He looked up to tell his friends to go away and was astonished to see the orange creature! He had no idea that it had been following him.

"What is that thing?" shrieked Runt, jumping away from the alien child. But Fish understood the creature's sounds: he said he was lost and wanted to find his parents. Chicken Little promised to help, but then a strange thing happened: there was a deafening rumble as the sky began to crack. Buck Cluck ran out to see what was happening. It really did seem as if...the sky was falling! In fact, it was an armada of spaceships made from panels that blended with the environment – just like the one that had fallen into Chicken Little's room. Now the spaceships were attacking Oakey Oaks!

As soon as he looked up and saw the sky splitting, the tiny alien started chattering excitedly. Fish translated the strange noises.

"Those are your parents?" Chicken Little asked in amazement. He realised that the aliens were coming for their son. The furry creature raced away, trying to reach his family.

"Watch out!" Chicken Little yelled to the panic-stricken people. "Don't hit the kid!" He chased after the baby alien and saw him stop in the middle of the road, unaware of the truck that was rumbling towards him. Chicken Little leaped on to a nearby car, bent back the aerial and launched himself through the air. He grabbed the alien child mid-flight and shot into the Oakey Oaks Theatre with him, landing on the stage in front of the screen.

"Chicken Little!" someone called from the back of the theatre. It was Buck!

Buck Cluck ran across the theatre to the stage, thankful that his son was safe.
"Son," he said, "you need to know that I love you, no matter what." The pair hugged
warmly, but then realised there was no time to lose. Chicken Little explained that
the alien needed to get back to its parents and his puzzled father agreed to help.
Outside, Chicken Little and his dad raced through the chaos. Aliens were zapping
cars and people, making them disappear. Mayor Turkey Lurkey offered the aliens the
key to the city, but with their green rays they zapped away the key, the Mayor's car,
and then the Mayor himself! Suddenly, the aliens saw their baby with Buck and
focused their rays on Buck, Chicken Little and the alien child. The three ducked into
a car while they thought up a new plan.

The little alien pointed to a spaceship above the Town Hall.

"Is that your parents?" asked Chicken Little. The alien nodded. "That's it, Dad!" shouted Chicken Little. "We get to the highest point on the Town Hall and give the kid back!"

Buck was nervous, but he trusted his son. With help from Runt, Fish and Abby, they rode across town in a fire engine and crashed into the Town Hall steps. Chicken Little and his father jumped off the truck with the alien and burst through the huge doors. They headed for the stairs and raced up them – all thirty flights! Coming out on to the roof, they climbed up to the dome and held the alien up for the spaceships to see.

"Here's your kid!" cried Chicken Little at the top of his voice. "Look over here!"

A spaceship hovered above the three, catching them in its giant beam.

After a burst of blinding light, Chicken Little and Buck suddenly found themselves floating in a dark chamber with the tiny alien. A huge screen flashed on in front of them, displaying three giant eyeballs that glared at them fiercely.

"WHY DID YOU TAKE OUR CHILD?" boomed a voice.

"You were the ones who left him behind!" Buck protested. "That's bad parenting...and I should know!"

"SILENCE!" roared the voice. "RELEASE THE CHILD!"

The little orange creature floated down and ran through a doorway into the arms of his happy mother, who carried him away. As he chattered away to her, they too appeared on the screen. He was safely home now, but the eyes still looked angry.

"YOU HAVE VIOLATED INTERGALACTIC LAW 90210!" the voice growled.

"He says they helped him," interrupted the alien's mother. "I think there's been a misunderstanding."

Chicken Little and his father were soon outside the spaceship, chatting with the aliens. They looked harmless without the spider-like suits they had worn earlier. The mother explained how they came to Oakey Oaks every year to collect the best acorns in the galaxy.

"And sorry for the whole invasion thing," added the father, shaking Buck's hand. "But, hey, I'm a dad. You know how it is with your kids. When they need you, you do whatever it takes." Buck nodded in agreement and put his arm around his own son, Chicken Little.

The aliens made sure the town was back to normal before saying goodbye. As they boarded their ship, one of its panels fell off – and it looked just like the one that had fallen on Chicken Little's head! So it was true: the sky (or spaceship panels that looked like the sky) really had fallen on Chicken Little...twice!

AND NOW, KIM POSSIBLE, YOUR FINAL *DEFEAT* IS AT HAND!

HANG ON, DOC. I GOTTA TAKE THIS.

BY ALL MEANS...

>bleep bleep<

KIM? IT'S *BONNIE.*

UH-OH.

THE SPRING DANCE COMMITTEE IS MEETING TONIGHT.

YOU *DO* HAVE THE *DECORATIONS* READY, DON'T YOU?

UHHH... NO PROBLEMO, BONNIE.

CAN'T TALK NOW, BUT I'LL SEE YOU TONIGHT.

LET'S WRAP THIS UP *FAST,* RON. I THINK BONNIE KNOWS I TOTALLY *FORGOT* ABOUT THE DANCE DECORATIONS!

BUT I *DO* HAVE A LITTLE SURPRISE PREPARED FOR MS. SHEGO, COURTESY OF *BUENO NACHO.*

READY?

I'M GOOD TO GO--AND SO IS *RUFUS!*

YOU THINK YOU'RE SUCH HOT STUFF, SO WHY NOT TRY A LITTLE *HOT SAUCE!*

SPLURT

AHHHH! THIS IS A *DESIGNER* TOP!

IF THAT STAINS, I'LL...

YOU'LL NEED YOUR HANDS FREE TO CLEAN UP THAT *MESS!*

THWAKK

63

DOC, AREN'T THE BARS OF 626'S CELL MADE OF THE **SAME** METAL YOU USED FOR THE BEAMS IN THAT LAST **TEST**?

YES, YES, YES-- WHAT IS YOUR **POINT**, 625?

AH, YES-- IT WILL **NEVER** HOLD HIM! NO CELL ON THE **PLANET** COULD!

I MUST FIND A WAY TO USE HIS POWER **AGAINST** HIM...

SKREEEK

OF COURSE! IT'S SO **SIMPLE**!

626 IS INCREDIBLY STRONG, BUT HIS BODY IS ALSO INCREDIBLY **HEAVY**!

SO, YOU'RE SAYING HE'S A **SINKER**?

LIKE A **STONE**!

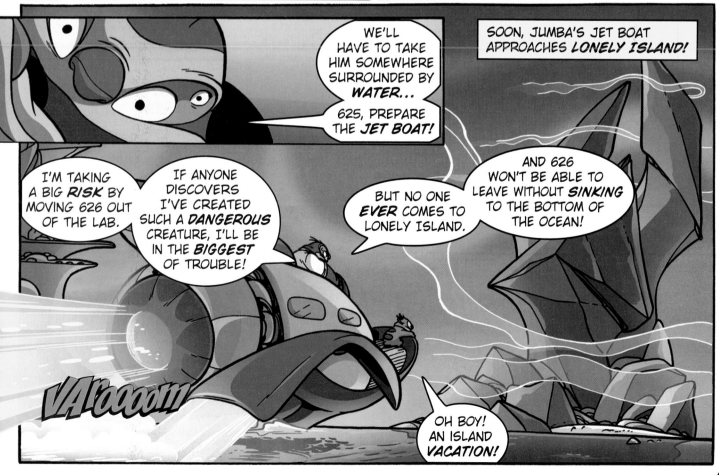

WE'LL HAVE TO TAKE HIM SOMEWHERE SURROUNDED BY **WATER**...

625, PREPARE THE **JET BOAT**!

SOON, JUMBA'S JET BOAT APPROACHES **LONELY ISLAND**!

I'M TAKING A BIG **RISK** BY MOVING 626 OUT OF THE LAB.

IF ANYONE DISCOVERS I'VE CREATED SUCH A **DANGEROUS** CREATURE, I'LL BE IN THE **BIGGEST** OF TROUBLE!

BUT NO ONE **EVER** COMES TO LONELY ISLAND.

AND 626 WON'T BE ABLE TO LEAVE WITHOUT **SINKING** TO THE BOTTOM OF THE OCEAN!

VAROOOOM

OH BOY! AN ISLAND **VACATION**!

STILL QUIET BACK THERE, DOC.

HE *LOVES* THOSE SANDWICHES I MADE.

THAT'S A *SURE* SIGN HOW SMART HE IS!

-GOBBLE-

-MUNCH-

BETTER STEP ON IT, THOUGH.

WHO KNOWS HOW LONG THE FOOD WILL KEEP HIM *QUIET*--

--YOU CAN *NEVER* TELL WHAT'S GOING TO SET THAT LITTLE GUY OFF...

SOON...

THIS ISN'T EXACTLY THE ISLAND *PARADISE* I WAS HOPING FOR, DOC.

THAT'S PRECISELY WHY NO ONE WILL *EVER* FIND US HERE.

626 IS SMART, BUT JUMBA IS *SMARTER!*

INSIDE...

SKREE

66

GET THE *MONITORING* DEVICE FROM THE BOAT.

I WANT IT SET UP BEFORE WE RELEASE 626.

UH... I THINK HE RELEASED *HIMSELF*, DOC.

FIND HIM!

HE MUSTN'T BE ALLOWED TO RUN *LOOSE* UNTIL WE LEAVE!

LOOKS LIKE HE WENT *THAT* WAY...

SANDWICH CRUMBS! HIS APPETITE HAS *BETRAYED* HIM!

626 IS CLEVER, BUT HE'LL *NEVER* OUTWIT HIS OWN CREATOR!

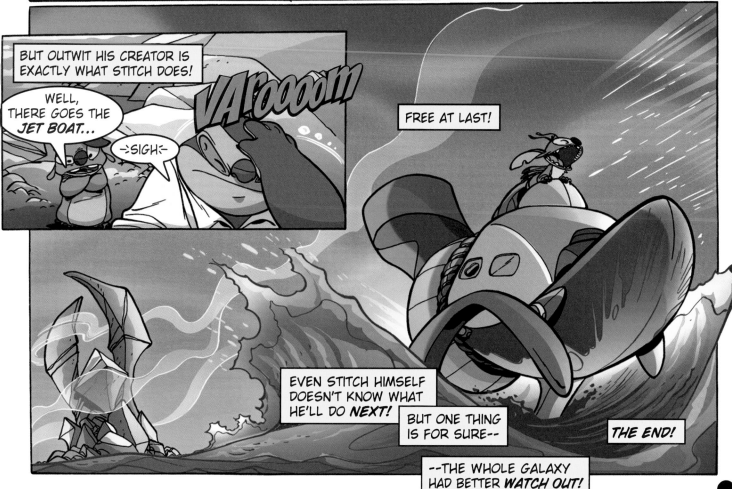

BUT OUTWIT HIS CREATOR IS EXACTLY WHAT STITCH DOES!

WELL, THERE GOES THE *JET BOAT*...

-:SIGH:-

VARooooom

FREE AT LAST!

EVEN STITCH HIMSELF DOESN'T KNOW WHAT HE'LL DO *NEXT!*

BUT ONE THING IS FOR SURE--

THE END!

--THE WHOLE GALAXY HAD BETTER *WATCH OUT!*

Aladdin's magical mysteries

So you think you know everything there is to know about the lad with the lamp? Find out how much of a genie genius you are with this spellbinding crossword!

DOWN

1 This parrot's squawk is worse than its bite (4)
2 Where Aladdin's fate is held by a thread (4,2,7)
3 The Genie has lived in this place for over 10,000 years (4)
4 Aladdin's way of floating around (5,6)
5 The name of the princess's loveable feline friend (5)
7 The colour of the Genie (4)
9 Aladdin's evil enemy (5)
10 The roly-poly ruler of Aladdin's city (6)
11 The Cave of Wonders is full of this (8)
15 You have to do this to the lamp to call the Genie (3)

ACROSS

4 The place where Aladdin and Jasmine first met (6)
6 The city where Aladdin lives (7)
8 Robin _ _ _ _ _ _ _ _ provides the voice of the Genie in the film (8)
9 The sultan's daughter (7)
12 The sultan lives in one of these (6)
13 Picture-clue A (5)
14 The princess's pet (5)
16 The baddie uses this magical tool to hypnotise his victims (5)
17 Picture-clue B (3)

A

B

ANSWERS Down 1 Iago 2 Cave of Wonders 3 lamp 4 magic carpet 5 Rajah 7 blue 9 Jafar 10 Sultan 11 treasure 15 rub Across 4 market 6 Agrabah 8 Williams 9 Jasmine 12 palace 13 Genie 14 tiger 16 staff 17 Abu

68

Disney's Aladdin

The bustling streets and alleyways of Agrabah, city of mystery and enchantment, hold the secrets of the story of Aladdin. His tale is one of a poor street boy and an ordinary-looking lamp. Neither one of them was what they seemed...

How was the course of this boy's life changed forever? Aladdin's story begins on a dark night in the desert, where a dark man waited with a dark purpose...

Jafar waited impatiently beneath the starlit sky. He pounced on a second man, Gazeem, who appeared from the shadows, and snatched something from his hand. He held it up: it was one half of a scarab beetle shape. From his own pocket, he took the other half and fitted the pieces together. Immediately, the scarab began to glow, then flew off into the sand. On the spot where it landed, a huge cave in the shape of a tiger's head sprang up in a swirl of sand.

"Go in and bring me the lamp," Jafar ordered. Gazeem tried, but was hurled back from the cave's entrance by a mighty roar from inside: "Only one may enter here, one whose worth lies far within – a diamond in the rough!"

To Jafar's horror, the cave then sank back into the sand. "I must find this diamond in the rough," he hissed.

Aladdin was a poor teenage boy who lived in the city of Agrabah. He was sometimes so hungry that he would have to steal food from market stalls. If the Sultan's guards saw him, they would chase him through the narrow streets, but Aladdin was much too quick and much too clever to be caught.

"Gotta eat to live, gotta steal to eat!" he would shout cheerfully to astonished passers by. He was, though, determined not to be a thief forever. As he gazed across the city at the Sultan's Palace one night, he made a promise to his pet monkey: "One day, Abu, things are going to change. We'll be rich and live in a palace. All our problems will be over." He smiled as he realised Abu had fallen asleep. It didn't matter; he would still keep his promise.

The next morning, there was trouble at the Sultan's Palace. Another prince had come to ask the Sultan's beautiful daughter to marry him, but he was chased away by her pet tiger. The Sultan demanded an explanation.

"Oh, Rajah was only playing," teased Princess Jasmine, fondly stroking her pet. She tried not to giggle as she noticed a piece of the fleeing prince's trousers in Rajah's mouth. The Sultan had no idea what to do. The law of the land stated that Jasmine should be married to a prince by her next birthday, but she had not liked any of the princes so far and there were only three days left.

"You've got to stop rejecting every prince who comes to call!" cried the Sultan.

Jasmine turned away sadly and stroked one of her doves.

"If I do marry," she told her father firmly, "it will be for love."

The Sultan stomped off, bumping into Jafar. "Ah, Jafar! My trusty adviser," he smiled. "My daughter refuses to choose a husband. What am I to do?"

"I have a solution, master," smirked Jafar, "but it requires your Mystique Blue Diamond."

"My ring?" spluttered the Sultan, taken aback. "But...but..." Before he could protest, Jafar held up his magic staff and used it to hypnotise the Sultan, sternly ordering him to hand over the diamond.

"Whatever you need," agreed the Sultan, dazed. Jafar hurried off into the depths of the Palace and placed the ring between the teeth of a pair of bronze snakes that held an hourglass. The sand inside began to swirl and an image of Aladdin appeared.

"Aha," snarled Jafar. "There he is! The only one who can enter the cave: the diamond in the rough. I shall ask the guards to invite him to the Palace..."

While Jafar made his evil plans, Jasmine decided that she was fed up of being a princess. She put on a plain cloak and escaped over the palace walls. Taking a deep breath, she hurried into the city and tried to lose herself amongst the market crowds. Being a princess, though, she did not know how to behave: she took an apple without paying for it and was accused of being a thief. Luckily for her, Aladdin rescued her from the angry fruit seller and whisked her away to the safety of his rooftop. Just as they were getting to know one another, the guards burst in and arrested him.

"Release him, by the order of the Princess!" cried Jasmine, throwing back her hood. She was astonished to be told that the guards' orders had come from Jafar and watched helplessly as Aladdin was carried off to the palace dungeons.

Imprisoned in a grimy cell, Aladdin was thinking about the beautiful girl he had just met. He knew he would not see her again: the law said she had to marry a prince and he was just a 'street rat'.

"I'm a fool!" he told himself angrily.

"You're only a fool if you give up, boy," came a voice from the darkness. A hunched old beggar hobbled towards Aladdin. "I'm a poor prisoner like yourself," he croaked, "but together we could be more."

The man told Aladdin about a cave of wonders that held treasure beyond his wildest dreams. He promised to share the riches if Aladdin went in to get a golden lamp.

"But it's out there and we're in here," Aladdin pointed out.

"Things are not always what they seem," cackled the old man, tapping a wall panel so that it slid away.

The beggar, of course, was Jafar in disguise. He led Aladdin through the desert and told him to go inside the cave. At the cave's mouth, Aladdin was stopped in his tracks by a roar from within that asked: "Who disturbs my slumber?"

"It is I, Aladdin," he replied, a little afraid.

"Proceed. Touch nothing but the lamp," warned the voice. As Aladdin crept down the steps, he heard the beggar reminding him to bring out the lamp if he wanted his reward. Reaching the bottom of the long staircase, he gasped when he saw the mountains of golden treasures piled up around him.

"Would you look at that!" he whispered to Abu. "Just a handful of this would make me richer than the Sultan!" He chuckled as a friendly magic carpet scurried round them.

"Maybe you can help us," smiled Aladdin. "We're looking for the lamp."

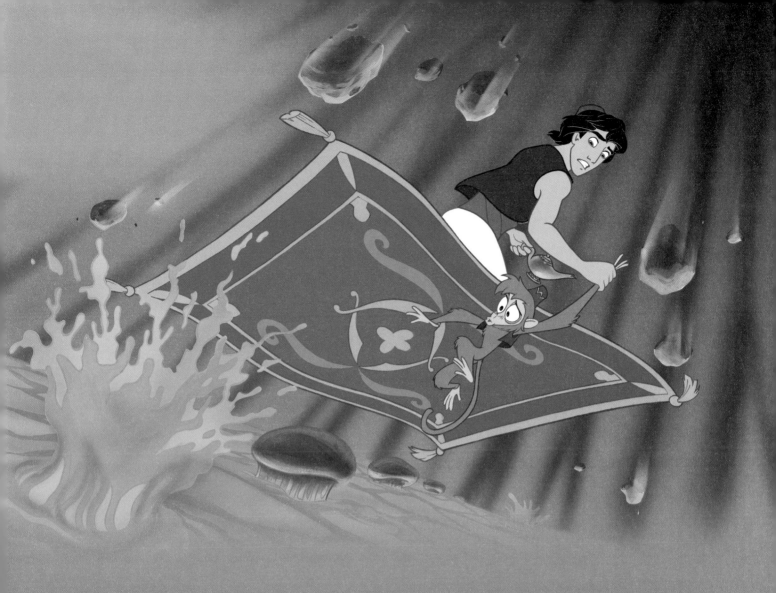

Aladdin followed the carpet and kept his promise not to touch anything. At last, he could see the lamp perched high on an enormous rock pedestal. Leaving Abu to admire the jewels, he climbed up the many steps to the top.

"Is this it?" he frowned, disappointedly peering at the ordinary-looking lamp. Before he could complain any more, he was startled by a deafening rumble. He turned to see that Abu had picked up a giant ruby. Grabbing the lamp, he went to run down the stone steps, but they collapsed to make a stone slide. As he hurtled down it, he heard the cave roar again: "Infidels! You have touched the forbidden treasure...now you will never again see the light of day!"

As the ground beneath them turned to molten lava, the carpet whisked Aladdin and Abu through a shower of falling rocks to safety.

Once the noise had stopped, Aladdin realised that there was no way out and they were trapped inside.

"Well, at least we have the lamp," he sighed, picking it up. It was covered in hundreds of years' worth of dust. "It looks like a piece of beat-up junk," he said, rubbing the lamp clean with his hand. Immediately, it began to glow. An explosion of sparks and smoke sprang out of it and a huge blue genie emerged.

"Ten thousand years gives you such a crick in the neck!" he complained loudly. Aladdin and Abu watched, astonished, as the Genie twisted his head all the way round...twice. "Wow, does it feel good to be out of there," he grinned. "You're a lot smaller than my last master," he added, peering down at Aladdin. "Either than or I'm getting bigger." Aladdin did not understand: he had never been anyone's master.

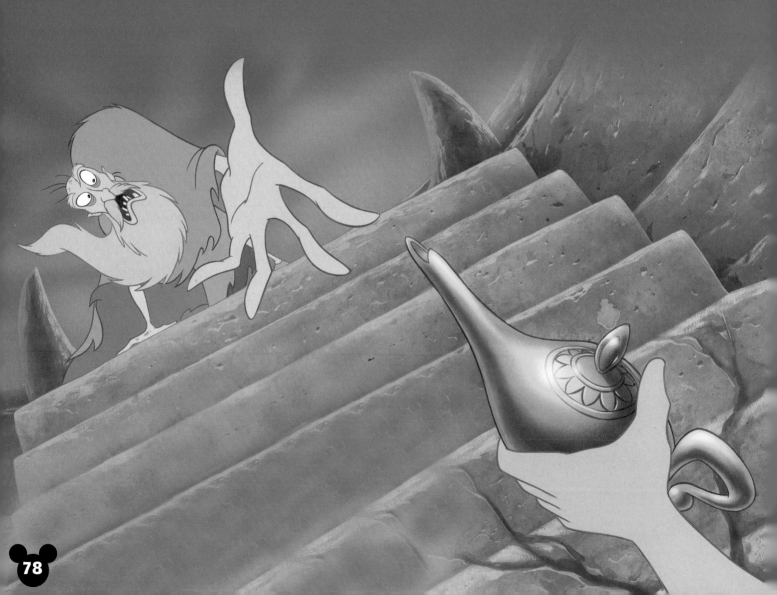

The Genie told Aladdin that he had three wishes. "But no wishing for more wishes!"
he chuckled. Seeing that Aladdin was still puzzled, he gave examples of what he
might ask for. He put on a breathtaking show, conjuring up a king's throne, dancing
girls, a tower of delicious fruit, piles of gold and an army of elephants.

"We pride ourselves on service," he told Aladdin, turning himself into a shop full of
barbers.

Now Aladdin understood. Being smart, he did not want to waste a wish on escaping.
He teased the Genie by betting that he could not free them, so within seconds they
were flying out of the cave's mouth and back across the desert.

Now Aladdin could make his first wish: to become a prince so that Jasmine might
marry him. Within seconds, he had been transformed into Prince Ali Ababwa.

Prince Ali Ababwa entered the city of Agrabah to the sound of a trumpet fanfare. Crowds cheered as his huge procession made its way to the Palace. Once inside, the Prince swooped up to the Sultan on his magic carpet and asked to see Jasmine. The Princess, however, refused to see him; she had met enough arrogant princes.

It was not until later that Aladdin managed to speak to Jasmine by climbing up to her balcony. He persuaded her to fly with him on the magic carpet and they soared through the starry sky over the city. Jasmine gasped as they sped on, past pyramids and sphinxes; she gazed in awe at the birds around her and gathered up bundles of fluffy clouds in her arms. At the end of a magical evening, she knew that she had met the man she would marry.

Jafar was furious; he had planned to make Jasmine marry him so that he could become Sultan. He ordered his men to tie up Prince Ali and throw him into the sea. As Aladdin lay on the seabed, the lamp rolled into his hands and the Genie appeared. He had no choice but to use Aladdin's second wish to save him from drowning.

Aladdin rushed back to the Palace, but before long Iago the parrot had stolen the lamp and taken it to Jafar. Now that Jafar was the Genie's master, he commanded him to make him Sultan. The Genie gave him his wish and picked up the palace to move it to a new position, towering over the city. Aladdin flew up to him on the carpet and pleaded with him to stop.

"Sorry, kid," he said sadly. "I've got a new master now."

Jasmine and her father refused to bow down before the new Sultan, so he used his second wish to become the most powerful sorcerer in the world. He showed everyone the real Aladdin and imprisoned Jasmine and her father in what was now his palace.

Aladdin was determined to outwit Jafar. He broke into the Palace and grabbed a sword, but Jafar used his sorcerer's magic to trap him inside a ring of fire. "Are you afraid to fight me yourself, you cowardly snake?" cried Aladdin. Jafar showed him just how snakelike he could be and turned himself into a giant serpent. Aladdin found the courage to mock him further and pointed out that the Genie was still the most powerful being. Jafar realised that Aladdin was right and used his final wish to become a genie. Aladdin's plan had worked: he grabbed the lamp and Jafar the Genie was sucked inside, imprisoned forever.

While the Genie hurled Jafar's lamp far into the desert, Aladdin freed Jasmine and her father. He then used his third wish to give the Genie the freedom that he had always wanted. The Genie was delighted and immediately announced that he was going to travel the world.

Aladdin tried to say sorry to Jasmine for pretending to be someone he wasn't, but she did not care that he was not a prince.

"The law's stupid!" she complained. "I love you!"

The Sultan could see how much his daughter cared for Aladdin. There was only one thing for it: he would change the law.

"From this day forth," he declared, "the Princess shall marry the man she chooses."

"I choose you...Aladdin," said Jasmine, hugging her husband-to-be. He had shown her a whole new world and now together, they would start a whole new life...

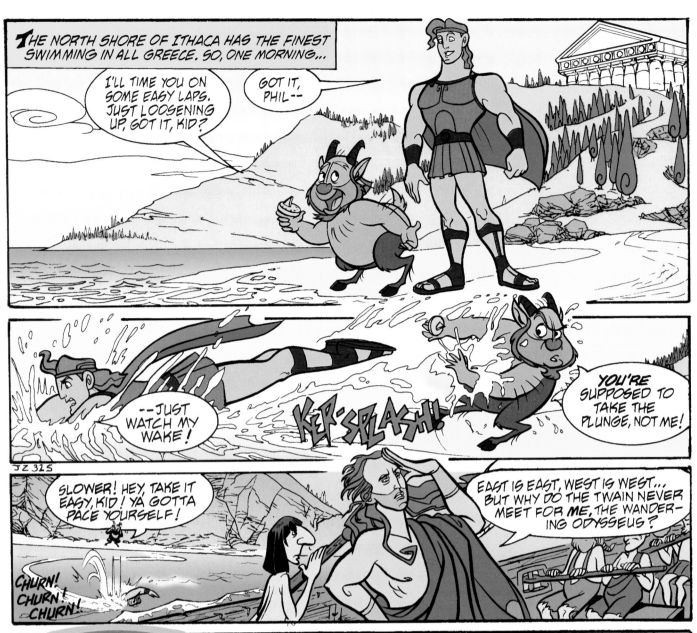

THE NORTH SHORE OF ITHACA HAS THE FINEST SWIMMING IN ALL GREECE. SO, ONE MORNING...

I'LL TIME YOU ON SOME EASY LAPS. JUST LOOSENING UP, GOT IT, KID?

GOT IT, PHIL--

--JUST WATCH MY WAKE!

KER-SPLASH!

YOU'RE SUPPOSED TO TAKE THE PLUNGE, NOT ME!

JZ 325

SLOWER! HEY, TAKE IT EASY, KID! YA GOTTA PACE YOURSELF!

CHURN! CHURN! CHURN!

EAST IS EAST, WEST IS WEST... BUT WHY DO THE TWAIN NEVER MEET FOR ME, THE WANDERING ODYSSEUS?

Disney's HERCULES in "ALL AT SEA"

HASN'T HE HEARD OF NORTH OR SOUTH?

DON'T CONFUSE HIM ANY MORE THAN HE ALREADY IS!

CLONK!

OW!

GOT IT!

CLEAR THE DECK, PLEASE. EXCUSE ME...

WHILE I PUT THIS BABY BACK WHERE IT BELONGS!

SHUNK

sheesh. HOW LONG HAS THIS KIND OF THING GONE ON?

OH, TEN OR TWENTY YEARS, I GUESS. BUT THIS LITTLE SQUALL WAS NOTHING...

YOU NAME IT, I'VE BEEN THROUGH IT. ONE CRISIS AFTER ANOTHER!

LET'S SEE. THERE WAS THE RUN-IN WITH THE CYCLOPS...THE TIME MY MEN TURNED TO SWINE...THE VISIT TO THE UNDERWORLD...THE ATTACK OF THE SIX-HEADED MONSTER...

AND SEVEN YEARS MAROONED WITH THE BEAUTIFUL CALYPSO! ACTUALLY, *THAT* WASN'T SO BAD--

WOW! WHAT COULD POSSIBLY BE LEFT?

LOOK! THE SIRENS!

U-U-UH OH-H-H! I D-DON'T THINK THIS M-MAST IS TOO SECURE--

SHUDDER

IN FACT, I'D SAY IT'S INSECURE! YIPE!

ZING!

WHOOSH!

YOU THINK THIS SCARES US, POSEIDON? FIE! I SPIT ON YOU!

THAT'S JUST A DROP IN THE OCEAN TO ME, PAL!

I BET I KNOW WHAT PHIL WOULD SAY RIGHT ABOUT NOW...

"USE YOUR HEAD, KID!"

SLAM!

OOF!!

WHEW! GOOD THING IT'S SAND. SOFT SAND?

SMAK! SMAK!

STILL, A LANDING LIKE THAT DOES KNOCK THE WAX OUT!

NOW *I'M* STRANDED. LOST ON A DESERT SHORE!

OH, WHY HAVE I BEEN *CURSED* SO? FATED TO WANDER ENDLESSLY...!

BETTER GET HOLD OF MYSELF. I'M STARTING TO SOUND LIKE YOU-KNOW-WHO

ODYSSEUS IS LUCKY. *HE'LL* PROBABLY MAKE IT HOME... EVENTUALLY...

HIYA, HERC!

MEG?

MEG? HOW DID YOU GET HERE?

PEGASUS FLEW ME. THIS IS WHERE WE ARRANGED TO MEET, REMEMBER?

ON THE SOUTH SHORE OF ITHACA, AT SUNSET!

NOW, DON'T TELL ME YOU'VE FORGOTTEN. WE MADE A DATE--

--TO GO SWIMMING!

!!

FLOMP!

NOW WHO PUT THE LEAD IN HIS HEADBAND? YOU'D THINK HE DIDN'T LIKE THE BEACH!

END

Duck's Luck!

Walt Disney's Cinderella

"Bibbidi-bobbidi-boo!"

With a short spell and a flourish of her shimmering wand, the fairy godmother transformed Cinderella's tattered dress into a beautiful ball gown. Cinderella was astonished: now she really could go to the ball! Her dream of meeting the Prince had been shattered once. As the fairy dust settled, she hoped it might finally come true...

Once upon a time in a faraway land, there lived a gentleman whose wife had died when their child was young. He doted on his only daughter and made sure she had the best of everything: beautiful dresses, a fine horse, a puppy to play with. They lived a comfortable life in their grand house with its pretty gardens, but he still felt that his little girl needed a mother. He chose a new wife who had her own daughters, Drizella and Anastasia: he hoped that the sisters would be playmates for his daughter.

Sadly, the girl's father became ill and died, leaving her to be cared for by her stepmother. It quickly became clear that the rest of the household were jealous of the pretty little orphan: her stepsisters were anything but playmates and treated her dreadfully, while her stepmother made her wear rags and do all the chores.

The girl became a servant in her own house and was forced to sleep in a tiny attic room overrun with mice. She would work a long day, fetching and carrying, scrubbing and cleaning. Before going to bed, she would huddle in the fire's dying cinders to get warm and for this was nicknamed Cinderella. Despite everything, she was still the gentle and kind girl she had always been. She made friends with the birds that woke her early each day and looked after the mice who shared her room, even making little clothes for them. The mice loved her, for she would rescue them from traps and protect them from her stepmother's bad-tempered cat, Lucifer.

In fact, Cinderella looked after every person and animal in the house. Each morning, she would prepare breakfast for the cat, the dog, the horse, the chickens, the geese, the ducks...and of course, her stepmother and stepsisters.

Even though Cinderella gave the mice all the food they needed, they always liked to try and get a little extra if they could. They would watch from an upstairs window as she scattered corn for the chickens around the yard and would sneak past Lucifer to try and get some. Gus, though, was not always as quick as the others. One morning, he was so busy trying to gather up more corn than he could carry that he didn't notice Lucifer right behind him. The sly cat pounced on him, but he managed to wriggle away and escape into the kitchen. With Lucifer at his heels, he scampered across the floor and up a table leg, taking cover under an upturned teacup.

"Cinderella!" came a shriek from upstairs. "Cinderella! Where's our cup of tea?"
Cinderella rushed in and filled the teapots, then added one to each of the tea trays.

It was such a long way from the kitchen to the bedrooms that Cinderella always tried to take all three trays in one trip. The only way to do this was to carry one in each hand and have the third on her head. She was so busy concentrating on her balancing act that she did not notice Lucifer skulking along behind her, his eyes fixed on the teacup that Gus was hiding beneath.

"Cinderella!" squawked Drizella impatiently. "Are you bringing my cup of tea?"

"I'm coming," Cinderella called back, keeping her head still as she climbed the long staircase and went into the first bedroom. She was delivering the third tray when she was startled by a shriek: Anastasia had discovered Gus under her teacup! The two sisters and their mother decided that Cinderella had put him there on purpose, so her punishment was a list of extra chores.

In the Royal Palace on the other side of town, the King was talking to the Grand Duke about his son.

"It's high time the Prince got married," he sighed. "If only he could meet the right girl." The King thought for a moment, then his face lit up.

"I have an idea!" he exclaimed. "We'll have a ball this evening and invite every girl in my kingdom. He's sure to fall in love with one of them."

The invitations were delivered by lunchtime. Cinderella politely thanked the royal servant who came to their door. With a puzzled frown, she broke the royal seal and read the invitation. Letting out an excited squeal, she took it to her stepmother.

"A ball! We're going to a ball!" sang Drizella and Anastasia, dancing joyfully with each other.

"I'm invited, too," Cinderella pointed out, just loud enough for them to hear.

The stepsisters laughed at the idea of Cinderella going to the royal ball.

"I see no reason why you can't go," said their mother, much to their surprise, "if you get all your work done and if you have a suitable dress to wear."

"IF," sniggered Anastasia and Drizella, realising her mother's game. They knew Cinderella would be too busy running round after them to get her chores done and she certainly had no dresses good enough to wear to a ball.

Anastasia and Drizella were right: Cinderella had only one decent dress and that needed an afternoon spending on it to make it right. Cinderella had to get three other dresses ready. Gus and his friends soon realised that she would never be able to do it, so they worked on it themselves, trimming it with ribbons from around the house and finding beads to go with it.

That evening, Cinderella came wearily up the dark stairs. She had managed to finish her chores, but thought she had no dress to wear. She gazed sadly out of her attic window at the Royal Palace in the distance, thinking she had missed her chance to meet the Prince.

"Surprise!" called her mice friends behind her. She gasped as she saw the beautiful gown and thanked them all eagerly. Changing into it as quickly as she could, she ran down as the others were about to leave.

" Wait!" she called. "I'm coming, too!"

The stepsisters spun round and glared jealously at Cinderella.

"You little thief!" screamed Drizella, snatching the beads from her. "They're mine!"

Anastasia then ripped a piece of ribbon from the dress, claiming it was hers. Before Cinderella could stop them, they had torn her gown to shreds while their mother looked smugly on.

Cinderella was heartbroken. She fled from the house into the garden and knelt before a bench in tears, giving up hope of ever going to the Palace. Suddenly, the dark garden was lit by a cloud of stardust and out of it emerged a kind-faced woman in a cloak.

"Dry those eyes, child," she said. "You can't go to the ball looking like that."

"Who are you?" whispered Cinderella, blinking away her tears.

"I'm your fairy godmother," came the reply, " and we don't have much time. Now, the first thing you'll need is a pumpkin."

Cinderella had no idea why she had to find a pumpkin, but she went and fetched one from the kitchen as she was told. Her fairy godmother waved her magic wand over it and with a 'Bibbidi-bobbidi-boo!' turned it into a magnificent carriage.

"Now we need some mice," smiled the fairy godmother.

Gus and his friends had come to see what was going on in the garden. Before they knew it, they had been turned into proud horses for the carriage. Cinderella's horse became the coachman and her dog was soon a footman. With a final wave of her wand, the fairy godmother gave Cinderella a stunning silken gown and sparkling glass slippers.

"You must leave the ball by midnight," the fairy godmother told Cinderella, as she stepped into the carriage. "On the last stroke of twelve, the spell will be broken." Promising not to stay later than twelve o'clock, Cinderella thanked her fairy godmother and waved goodbye. With a flick of the reigns, the coachman made the horses spring into action and soon they were trotting past the moonlit lake to the Royal Palace. The ball had already begun, but Cinderella would be there: she was happy at last.

Reaching the palace, Cinderella stepped nervously down from her carriage. She took a deep breath before sweeping gracefully up the steps and into the ballroom. The Prince was bowing to Anastasia and Drizella near the doorway. As he stood upright again, he caught sight of Cinderella and felt his heart leap: he had never seen such a beautiful girl. Ignoring the others who were trying to get his attention, he walked over to Cinderella, took her hand and led her to the centre of the grand ballroom.

The Prince refused to dance with anyone else for the rest of the evening and would not let go of Cinderella's hand for a moment. No one at the ball recognised her and they all wondered who the beautiful stranger might be. The King was delighted, for his plan had worked and his son had found the bride of his dreams.

The evening ended too soon as the clock began to strike midnight.

"I must go!" Cinderella cried, remembering her promise. She snatched her hand away from her dancing partner and ran across the ballroom. Taken aback, the Prince went after her.

"Wait!" he called from the palace entrance, but the glittering carriage sped away into the darkness. Crestfallen, the Prince made his way down the steps to pick up something his guest had dropped: it was a glass slipper. He held it up and smiled as the tiny shoe winked in the moonlight. If the beautiful stranger would not come back for it, then he would take it to her.

Some way away, Cinderella stood laughing in her ragged dress, her animal friends around her. She had almost managed to get home before the spell had broken and had a memento of her evening: a single glass slipper.

The next morning, the Prince let it be known that he wished to marry the girl whose foot would exactly fit the glass slipper. He sent the Grand Duke round the whole kingdom to try the shoe on each young woman until its owner was found.

Cinderella's stepmother was determined that one of her daughters would be the new Princess. To make sure that Cinderella did not get the chance to put on the slipper, she locked her in her room, just as the Grand Duke and footman arrived at the house.

"Oh, please, you must let me out!" cried Cinderella, rattling at the doorknob.

Watched by two of the mice, her stepmother merely hurried away to welcome her visitors at the door, slipping the key into her pocket.

"Do come in," she smiled, knowing that no one would hear Cinderella's cries from way up in the attic.

Neither Drizella nor Anastasia could squash her big foot into the glass slipper. While their mother was busy willing the shoe to fit, Gus and his friend Jaq took the key from her pocket.

"If there are no other ladies in the household, then we will bid you good day," said the Grand Duke, preparing to leave for the next house.

"Please wait, Your Grace," Cinderella called from the top of the stairs. "May I try the slipper?"

Cinderella's stepmother tried to block her path as she came down the stairs, but the Grand Duke insisted that he must see 'every maiden in the land'. Cinderella took a seat, but her desperate stepmother tripped up the footman before he could reach her. He tumbled over, dropping the slipper and shattering it. To everyone's surprise, Cinderella took an identical one from her apron pocket: of course, it fitted perfectly.

The Grand Duke was delighted. He whisked Cinderella away in the King's coach and took her to the Palace where she was reunited with the Prince. Wedding plans were quickly made and before long, the Palace bells were ringing out to celebrate Cinderella's wedding day. The King and the Grand Duke watched proudly as the Prince and his new wife waved to the rejoicing crowds from the Palace steps beneath a shower of confetti. The Prince had never been so happy and would be forever thankful that Cinderella had lost her shoe on the night of the ball.

The happiest person at the wedding was Cinderella herself. At last, her dreams had come true: she had a husband she loved and who loved her, and she had become a princess. Most important of all, she would never again have to be a servant to her stepmother, Drizella and Anastasia.

Duck's Luck!

Duck's Luck!